PLEASE WASH YOUR HANDS BEFORE YOU READ ME AND KEEP ME CLEAN

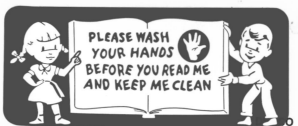

TRANSFORMERS: DEFIANCE
ISSUE NUMBER FOUR (OF FOUR)

WRITTEN BY: **CHRIS MOWRY**
PENCILS BY: **DAN KHANNA & ANDREW GRIFFITH**
INKS BY: **ANDREW GRIFFITH & JOHN WYCOUGH**
COLORS BY: **JOSH PEREZ**
LETTERS BY: **CHRIS MOWRY**
EDITS BY: **ANDY SCHMIDT & DENTON J. TIPTON**

Barely surviving a DECEPTICON ambush, the AUTOBOTS have gone into hiding. MEGATRON begins to understand more of what it is his new master has asked of him, including the construction of a massive space cruiser, the NEMESIS. With his new army growing in numbers, MEGATRON is set to conquer all that stands before him. But somewhere on CYBERTRON is a small group of fighters determined to restore order to the planet. With their ranks increasing, the AUTOBOT resistance is set to rally against MEGATRON alongside their new leader, OPTIMUS PRIME.

Special thanks to Hasbro's Aaron Archer, Michael Kelly, Amie Lozanski, Val Roca, Ed Lane, Michael Provost, Erin Hillman, Samantha Lomow, and Michael Verrecchia for their invaluable assistance.

To discuss this issue of ***Transformers***, join the IDW Insiders, or to check out exclusive Web offers, check out our site:

Spotlight

IDW

Licensed by:

Hasbro

DREAMWORKS PICTURES

Paramount

GM OFFICIAL LICENSED PRODUCT

WWW.IDWPUBLISHING.COM

VISIT US AT
www.abdopublishing.com

Reinforced library bound edition published in 2010 by Spotlight, a division of the ABDO Group, 8000 West 78th Street, Edina, Minnesota 55439. Published by agreement with IDW Publishing. www.idwpublishing.com

Printed in the United States of America, Melrose Park, Illinois.
102009
012010

 PRINTED ON RECYCLED PAPER

Library of Congress Cataloging-in-Publication Data

Mowry, Chris.
  Defiance / written by Chris Mowry ; pencils by Dan Khanna, Andrew Griffith, & Don Figueroa inks by Andrew Griffith & John Wycough ; colors by Josh Perez ; letters by Chris Mowry.
     v. cm.
  "Transformers, revenge of the fallen, offical movie prequel."
  ISBN 978-1-59961-721-3 (vol. 1) -- ISBN 978-1-59961-722-0 (vol. 2)
  ISBN 978-1-59961-723-7 (vol. 3) -- ISBN 978-1-59961-724-4 (vol. 4)
  1. Graphic novels. I. Transformers, revenge of the fallen (Motion picture) II. Title.
PZ7.7.M69De 2010
741.5'973--dc22
                          2009036394

All Spotlight books have reinforced library bindings and are manufactured in the United States of America.

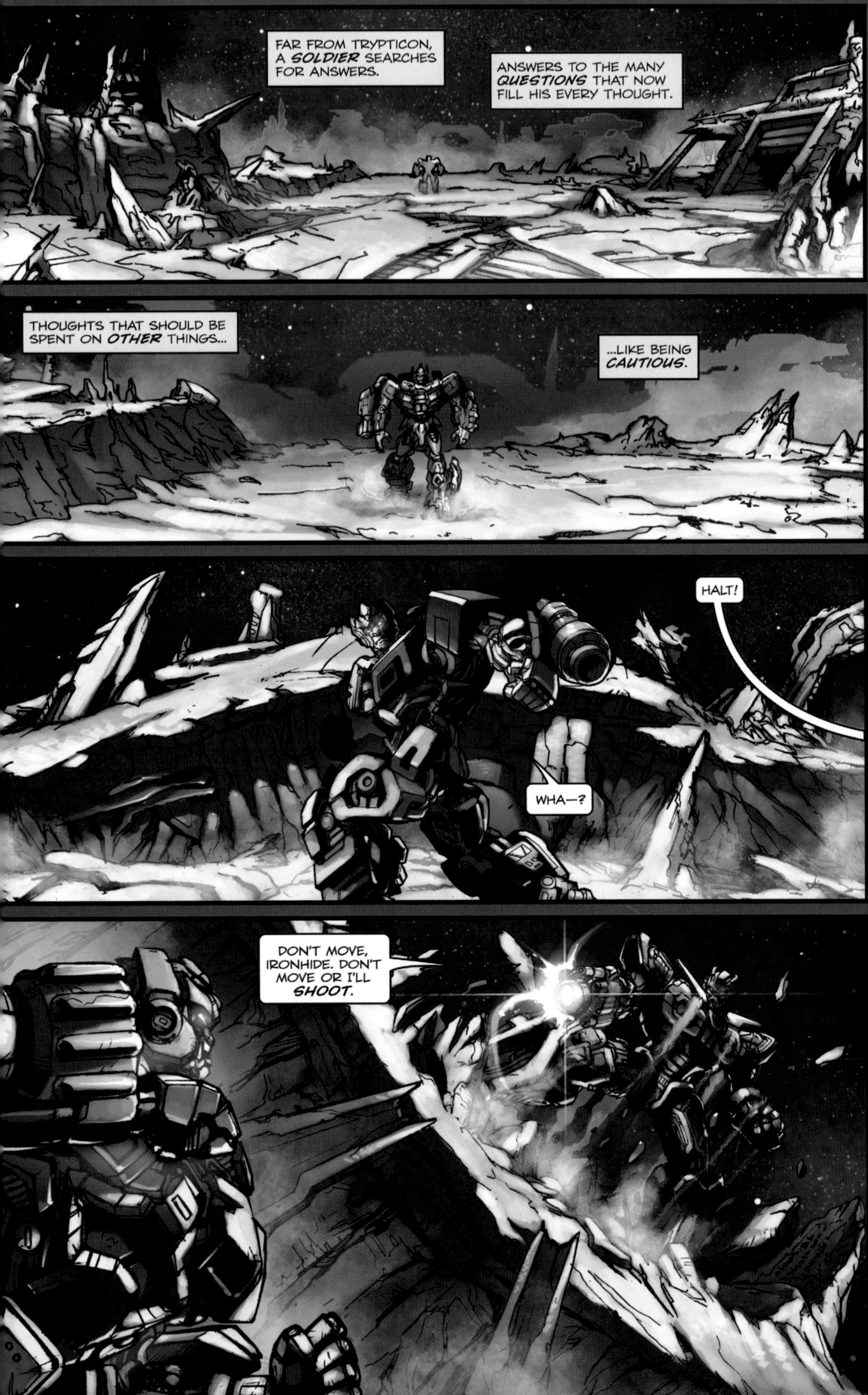
FAR FROM TRYPTICON, A SOLDIER SEARCHES FOR ANSWERS.
ANSWERS TO THE MANY QUESTIONS THAT NOW FILL HIS EVERY THOUGHT.
THOUGHTS THAT SHOULD BE SPENT ON OTHER THINGS...
...LIKE BEING CAUTIOUS.
HALT!
WHA—?
DON'T MOVE, IRONHIDE. DON'T MOVE OR I'LL SHOOT.

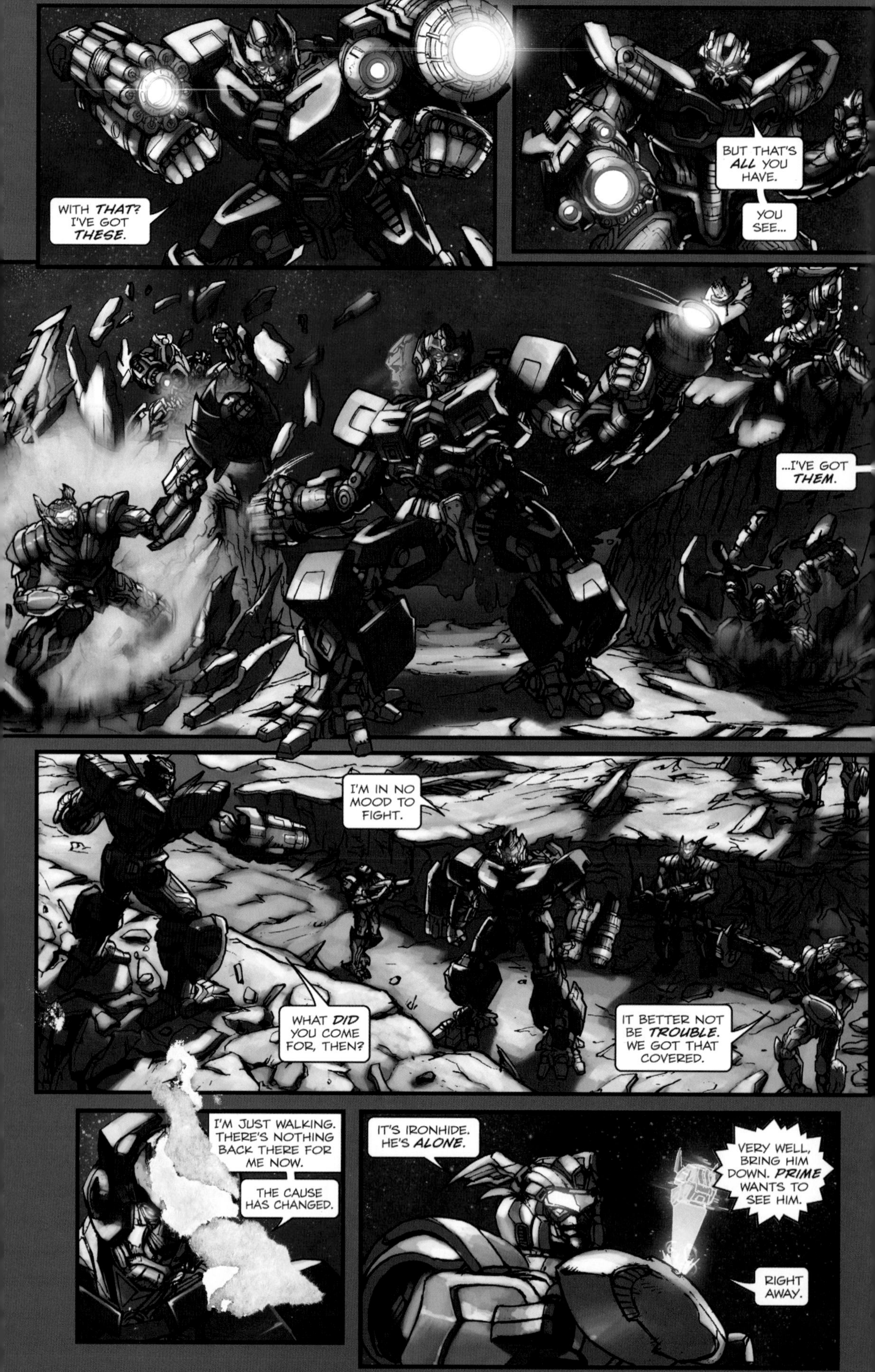
WITH THAT? I'VE GOT THESE.
BUT THAT'S ALL YOU HAVE.
YOU SEE...
...I'VE GOT THEM.
I'M IN NO MOOD TO FIGHT.
WHAT DID YOU COME FOR, THEN?
IT BETTER NOT BE TROUBLE. WE GOT THAT COVERED.
I'M JUST WALKING. THERE'S NOTHING BACK THERE FOR ME NOW.
THE CAUSE HAS CHANGED.
IT'S IRONHIDE. HE'S ALONE.
VERY WELL, BRING HIM DOWN. PRIME WANTS TO SEE HIM.
RIGHT AWAY.

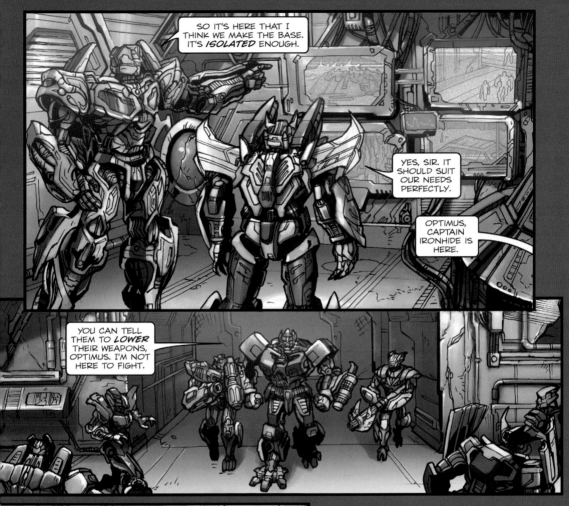

SO IT'S HERE THAT I THINK WE MAKE THE BASE. IT'S *ISOLATED* ENOUGH.

YES, SIR. IT SHOULD SUIT OUR NEEDS PERFECTLY.

OPTIMUS, CAPTAIN IRONHIDE IS HERE.

YOU CAN TELL THEM TO *LOWER* THEIR WEAPONS, OPTIMUS. I'M NOT HERE TO FIGHT.

THEN WHAT *ARE* YOU HERE FOR, IRONHIDE?

I'M HERE TO *JOIN* YOU.

YOU'LL *NEED* MY HELP, TOO.

MEGATRON IS FORMING AN ARMY, AND HE'S FINDING NO TROUBLE IN FILLING THE RANKS.

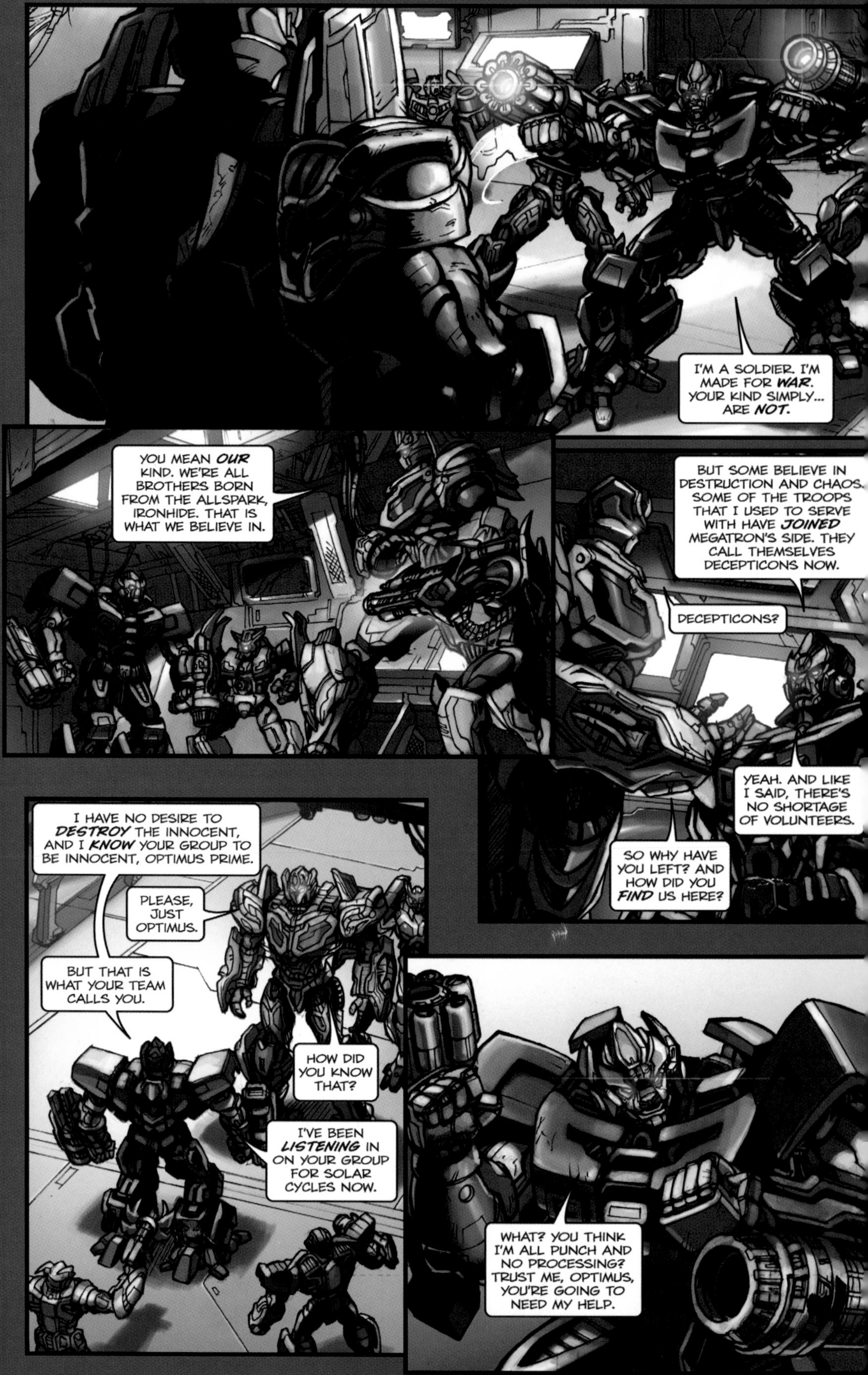
I'M A SOLDIER. I'M MADE FOR *WAR*. YOUR KIND SIMPLY... ARE *NOT*.
YOU MEAN *OUR* KIND. WE'RE ALL BROTHERS BORN FROM THE ALLSPARK, IRONHIDE. THAT IS WHAT WE BELIEVE IN.
BUT SOME BELIEVE IN DESTRUCTION AND CHAOS. SOME OF THE TROOPS THAT I USED TO SERVE WITH HAVE *JOINED* MEGATRON'S SIDE. THEY CALL THEMSELVES DECEPTICONS NOW.
DECEPTICONS?
YEAH. AND LIKE I SAID, THERE'S NO SHORTAGE OF VOLUNTEERS.
SO WHY HAVE YOU LEFT? AND HOW DID YOU *FIND* US HERE?
I HAVE NO DESIRE TO *DESTROY* THE INNOCENT, AND I *KNOW* YOUR GROUP TO BE INNOCENT, OPTIMUS PRIME.
PLEASE, JUST OPTIMUS.
BUT THAT IS WHAT YOUR TEAM CALLS YOU.
HOW DID YOU KNOW THAT?
I'VE BEEN *LISTENING* IN ON YOUR GROUP FOR SOLAR CYCLES NOW.
WHAT? YOU THINK I'M ALL PUNCH AND NO PROCESSING? TRUST ME, OPTIMUS, YOU'RE GOING TO NEED MY HELP.

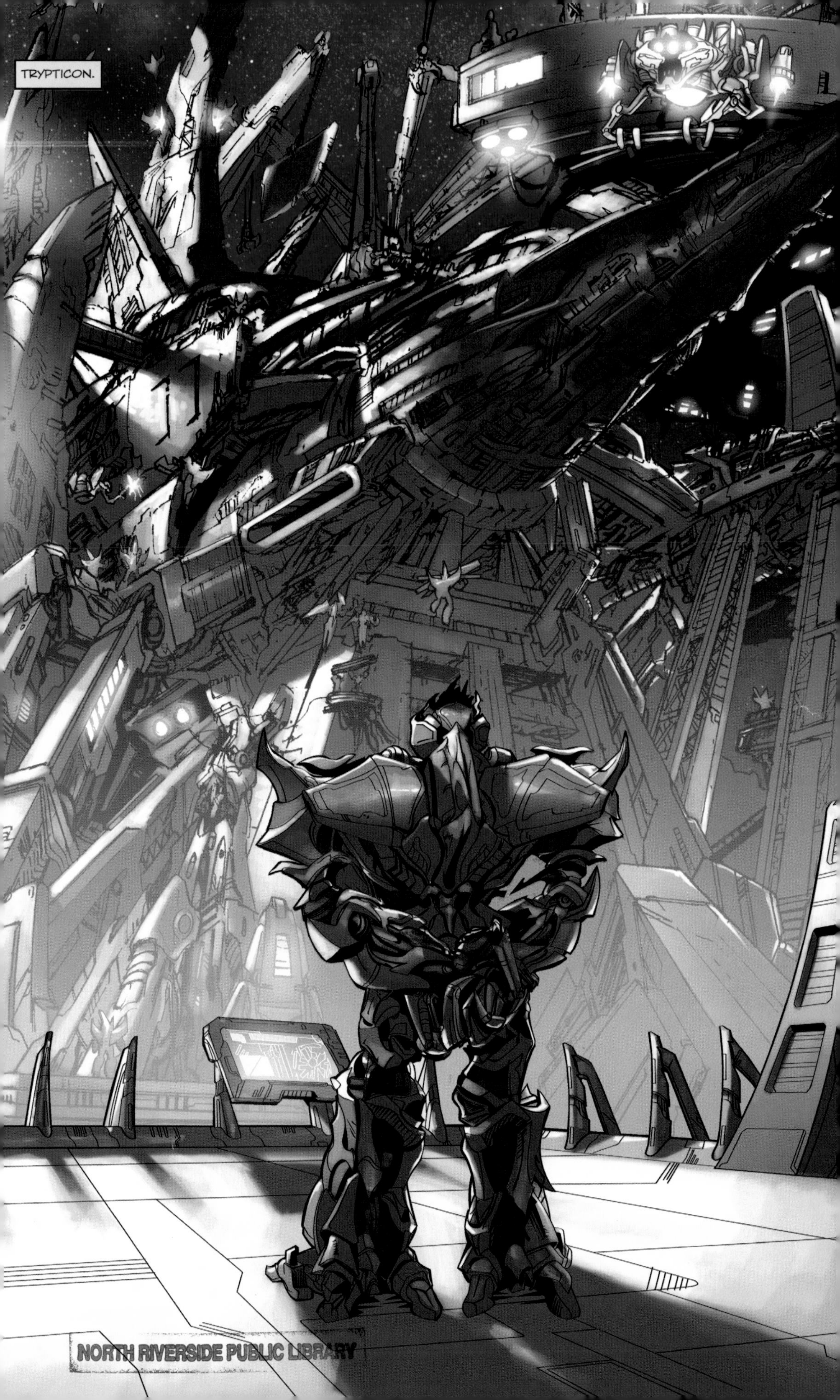
TRYPTICON.

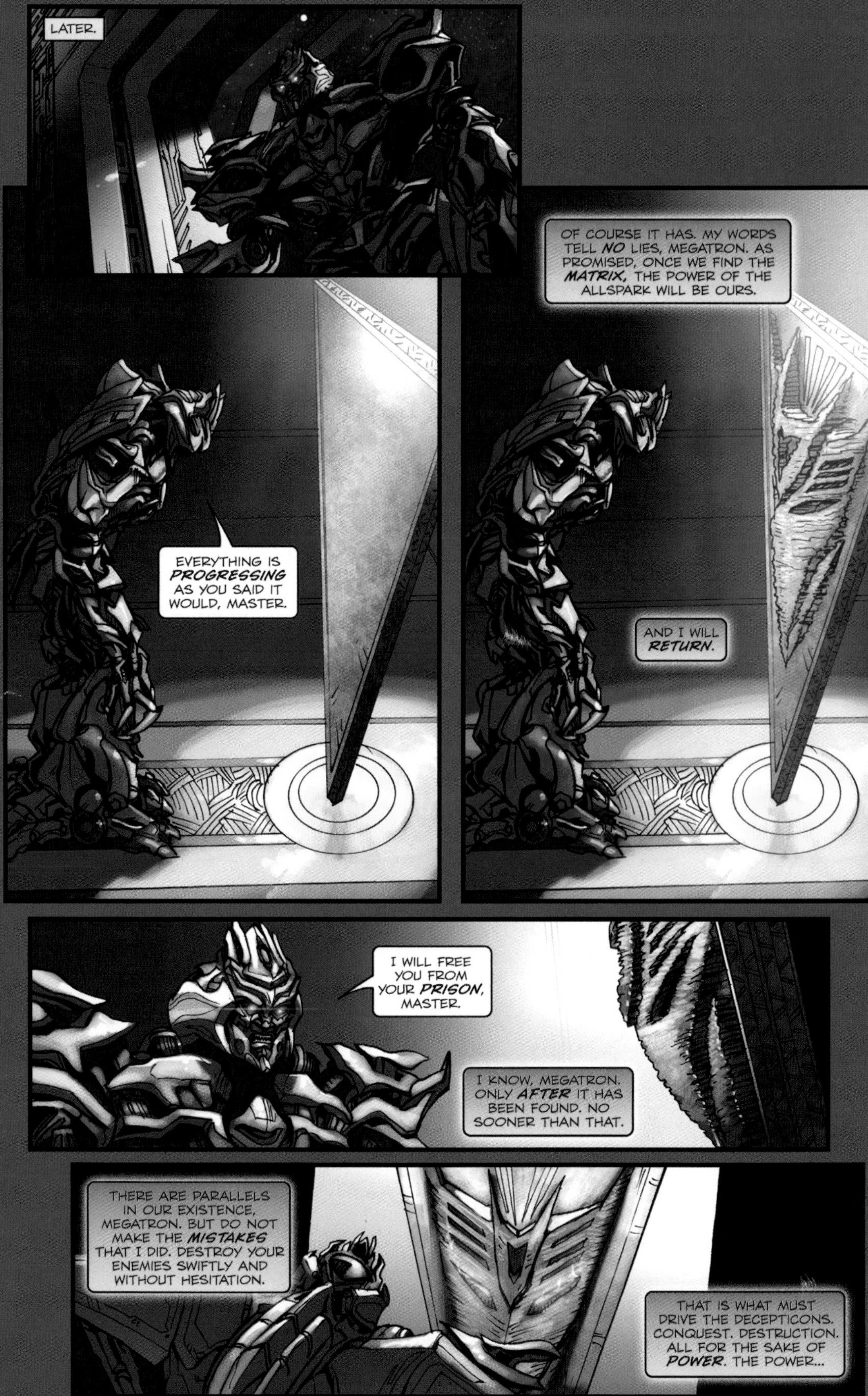

LATER.
EVERYTHING IS PROGRESSING AS YOU SAID IT WOULD, MASTER.
OF COURSE IT HAS. MY WORDS TELL NO LIES, MEGATRON. AS PROMISED, ONCE WE FIND THE MATRIX, THE POWER OF THE ALLSPARK WILL BE OURS.
AND I WILL RETURN.
I WILL FREE YOU FROM YOUR PRISON, MASTER.
I KNOW, MEGATRON. ONLY AFTER IT HAS BEEN FOUND. NO SOONER THAN THAT.
THERE ARE PARALLELS IN OUR EXISTENCE, MEGATRON. BUT DO NOT MAKE THE MISTAKES THAT I DID. DESTROY YOUR ENEMIES SWIFTLY AND WITHOUT HESITATION.
THAT IS WHAT MUST DRIVE THE DECEPTICONS. CONQUEST. DESTRUCTION. ALL FOR THE SAKE OF POWER. THE POWER...

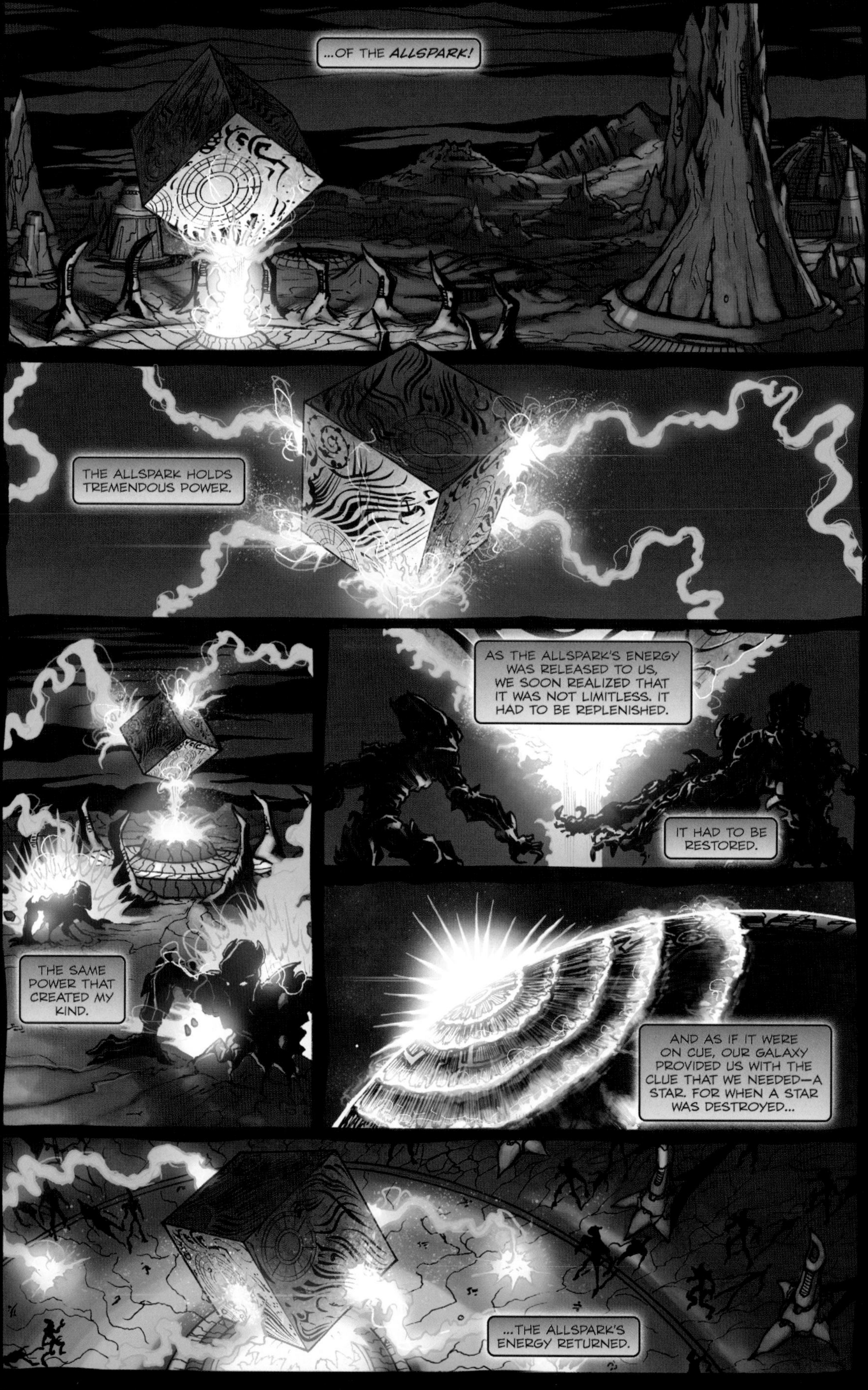
...OF THE ALLSPARK!
THE ALLSPARK HOLDS TREMENDOUS POWER.
THE SAME POWER THAT CREATED MY KIND.
AS THE ALLSPARK'S ENERGY WAS RELEASED TO US, WE SOON REALIZED THAT IT WAS NOT LIMITLESS. IT HAD TO BE REPLENISHED.
IT HAD TO BE RESTORED.
AND AS IF IT WERE ON CUE, OUR GALAXY PROVIDED US WITH THE CLUE THAT WE NEEDED—A STAR. FOR WHEN A STAR WAS DESTROYED...
...THE ALLSPARK'S ENERGY RETURNED.

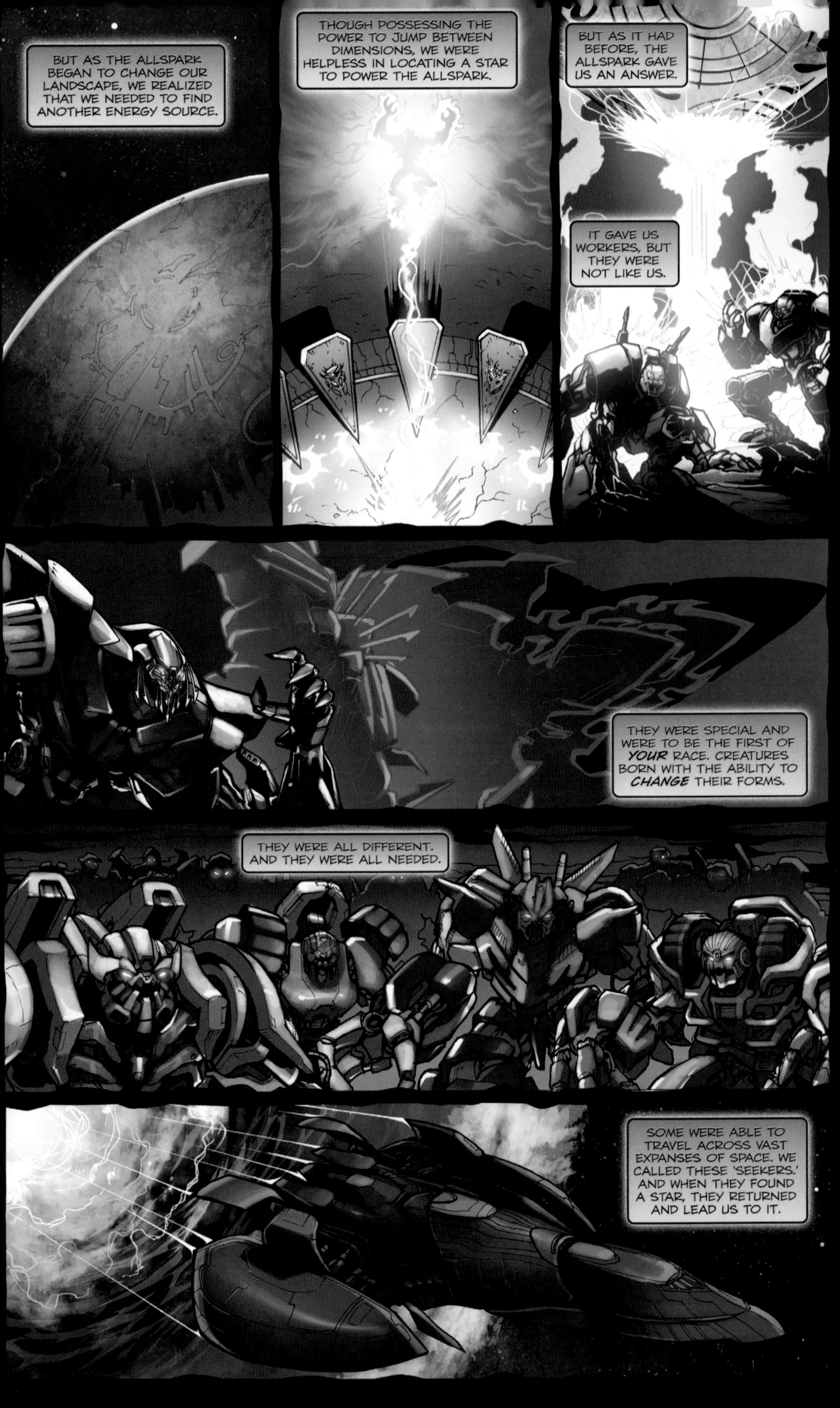
BUT AS THE ALLSPARK BEGAN TO CHANGE OUR LANDSCAPE, WE REALIZED THAT WE NEEDED TO FIND ANOTHER ENERGY SOURCE.
THOUGH POSSESSING THE POWER TO JUMP BETWEEN DIMENSIONS, WE WERE HELPLESS IN LOCATING A STAR TO POWER THE ALLSPARK.
BUT AS IT HAD BEFORE, THE ALLSPARK GAVE US AN ANSWER.
IT GAVE US WORKERS, BUT THEY WERE NOT LIKE US.
THEY WERE SPECIAL AND WERE TO BE THE FIRST OF YOUR RACE. CREATURES BORN WITH THE ABILITY TO CHANGE THEIR FORMS.
THEY WERE ALL DIFFERENT. AND THEY WERE ALL NEEDED.
SOME WERE ABLE TO TRAVEL ACROSS VAST EXPANSES OF SPACE. WE CALLED THESE 'SEEKERS.' AND WHEN THEY FOUND A STAR, THEY RETURNED AND LEAD US TO IT.

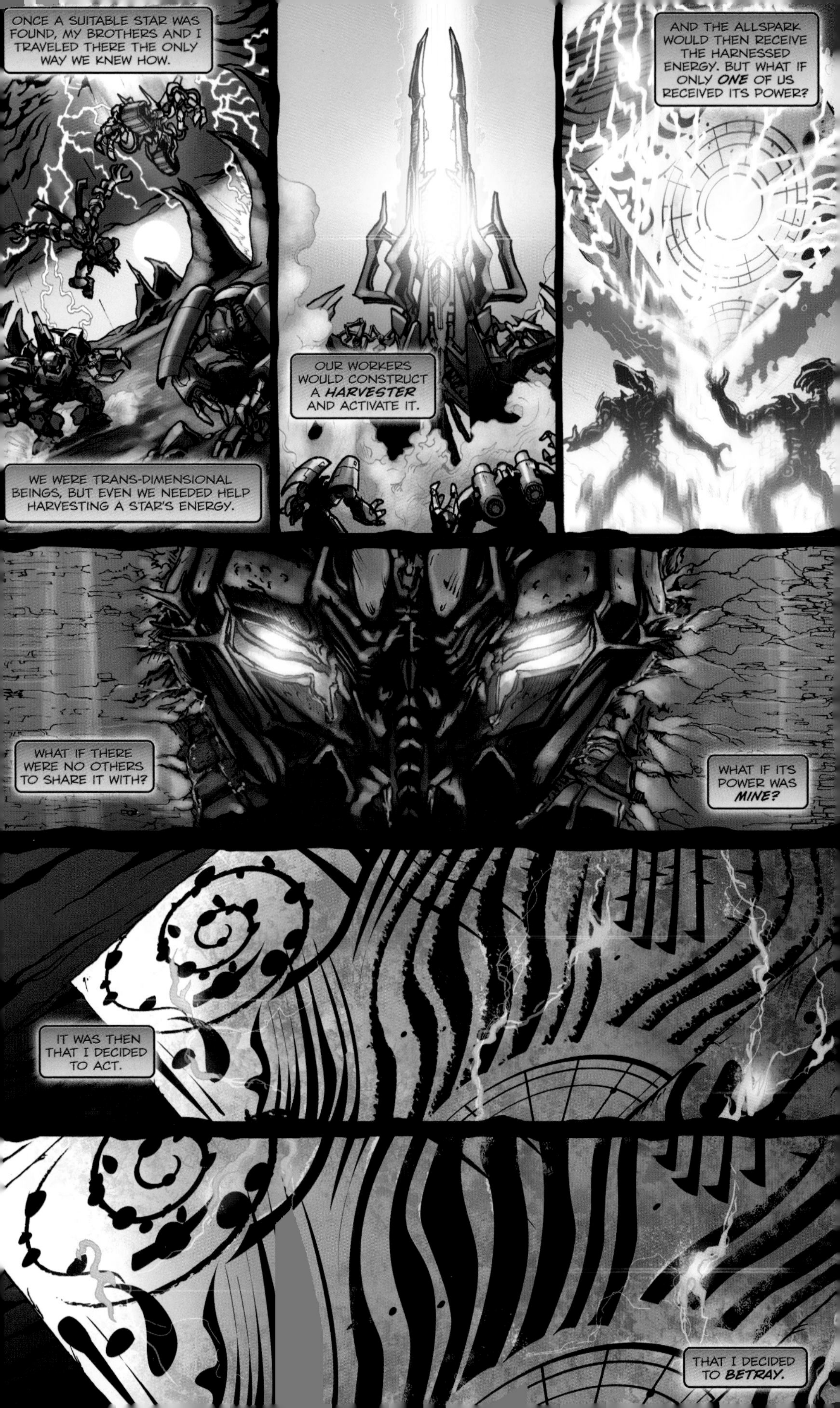
ONCE A SUITABLE STAR WAS FOUND, MY BROTHERS AND I TRAVELED THERE THE ONLY WAY WE KNEW HOW.
WE WERE TRANS-DIMENSIONAL BEINGS, BUT EVEN WE NEEDED HELP HARVESTING A STAR'S ENERGY.
OUR WORKERS WOULD CONSTRUCT A **HARVESTER** AND ACTIVATE IT.
AND THE ALLSPARK WOULD THEN RECEIVE THE HARNESSED ENERGY. BUT WHAT IF ONLY **ONE** OF US RECEIVED ITS POWER?
WHAT IF THERE WERE NO OTHERS TO SHARE IT WITH?
WHAT IF ITS POWER WAS **MINE?**
IT WAS THEN THAT I DECIDED TO ACT.
THAT I DECIDED TO **BETRAY.**

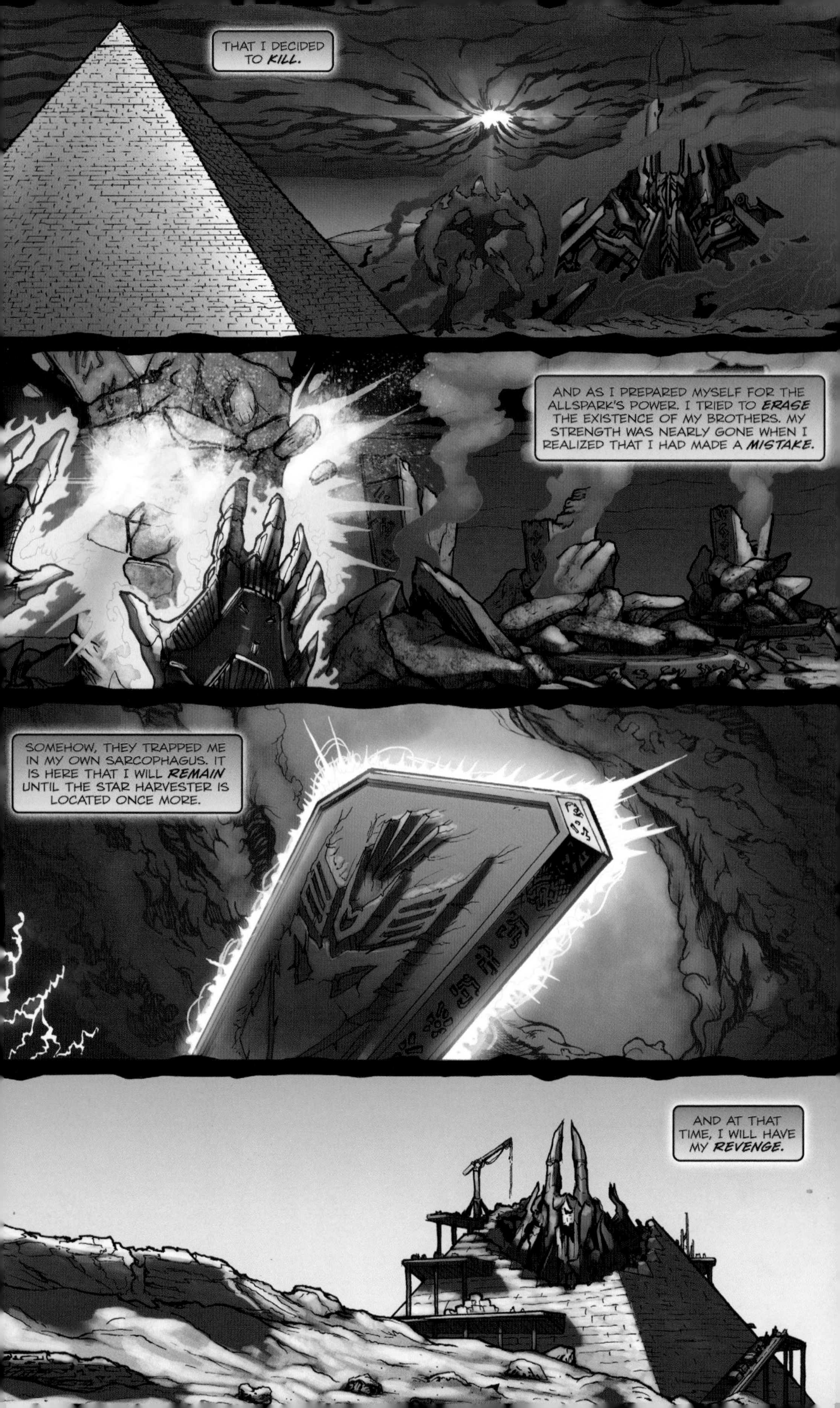

THAT I DECIDED TO KILL.
AND AS I PREPARED MYSELF FOR THE ALLSPARK'S POWER. I TRIED TO ERASE THE EXISTENCE OF MY BROTHERS. MY STRENGTH WAS NEARLY GONE WHEN I REALIZED THAT I HAD MADE A MISTAKE.
SOMEHOW, THEY TRAPPED ME IN MY OWN SARCOPHAGUS. IT IS HERE THAT I WILL REMAIN UNTIL THE STAR HARVESTER IS LOCATED ONCE MORE.
AND AT THAT TIME, I WILL HAVE MY REVENGE.

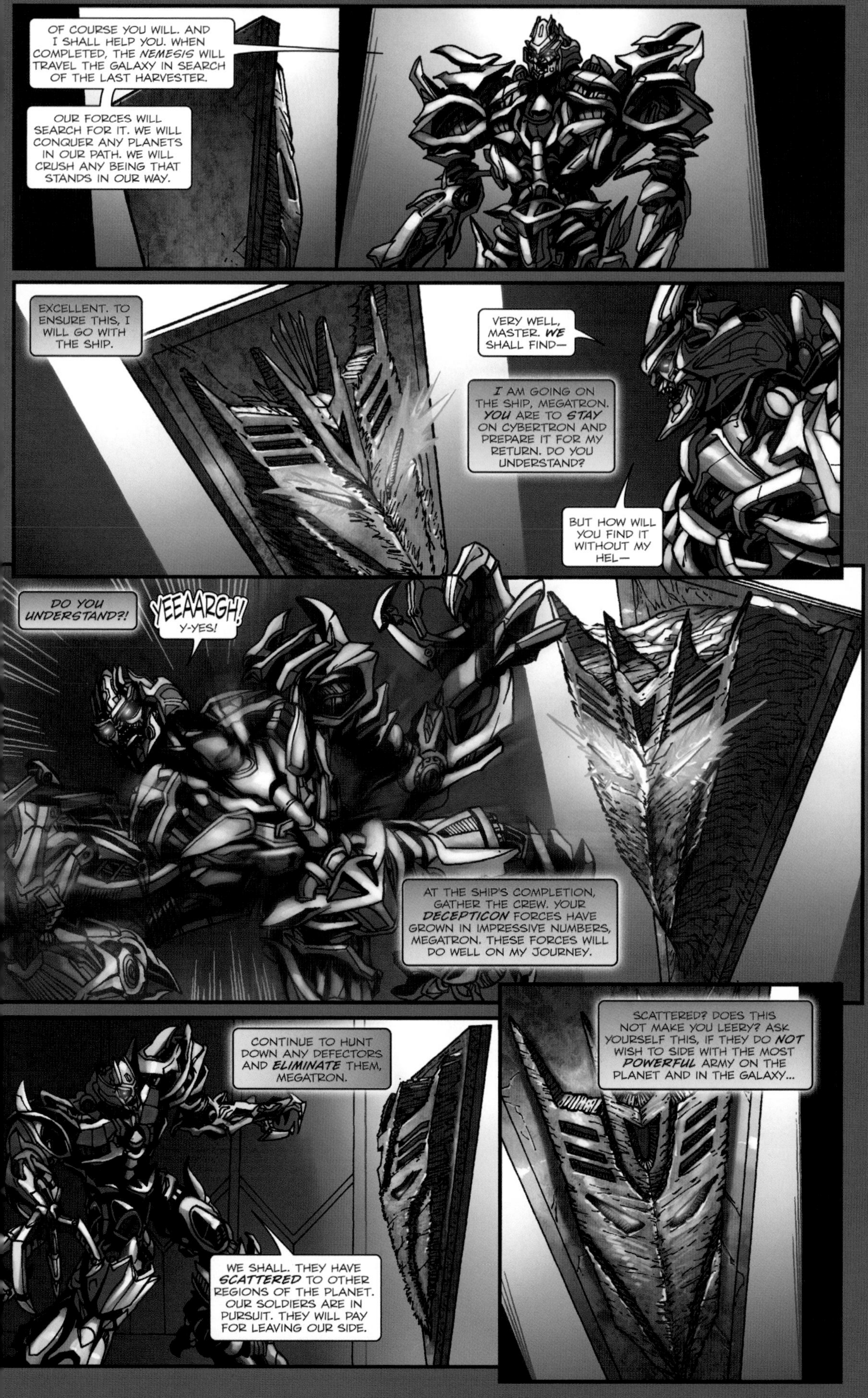
OF COURSE YOU WILL. AND I SHALL HELP YOU. WHEN COMPLETED, THE NEMESIS WILL TRAVEL THE GALAXY IN SEARCH OF THE LAST HARVESTER.
OUR FORCES WILL SEARCH FOR IT. WE WILL CONQUER ANY PLANETS IN OUR PATH. WE WILL CRUSH ANY BEING THAT STANDS IN OUR WAY.
EXCELLENT. TO ENSURE THIS, I WILL GO WITH THE SHIP.
VERY WELL, MASTER. WE SHALL FIND—
I AM GOING ON THE SHIP, MEGATRON. YOU ARE TO STAY ON CYBERTRON AND PREPARE IT FOR MY RETURN. DO YOU UNDERSTAND?
BUT HOW WILL YOU FIND IT WITHOUT MY HEL—
DO YOU UNDERSTAND?!
YEEAAARGH!
Y-YES!
AT THE SHIP'S COMPLETION, GATHER THE CREW. YOUR DECEPTICON FORCES HAVE GROWN IN IMPRESSIVE NUMBERS, MEGATRON. THESE FORCES WILL DO WELL ON MY JOURNEY.
CONTINUE TO HUNT DOWN ANY DEFECTORS AND ELIMINATE THEM, MEGATRON.
WE SHALL. THEY HAVE SCATTERED TO OTHER REGIONS OF THE PLANET. OUR SOLDIERS ARE IN PURSUIT. THEY WILL PAY FOR LEAVING OUR SIDE.
SCATTERED? DOES THIS NOT MAKE YOU LEERY? ASK YOURSELF THIS, IF THEY DO NOT WISH TO SIDE WITH THE MOST POWERFUL ARMY ON THE PLANET AND IN THE GALAXY...

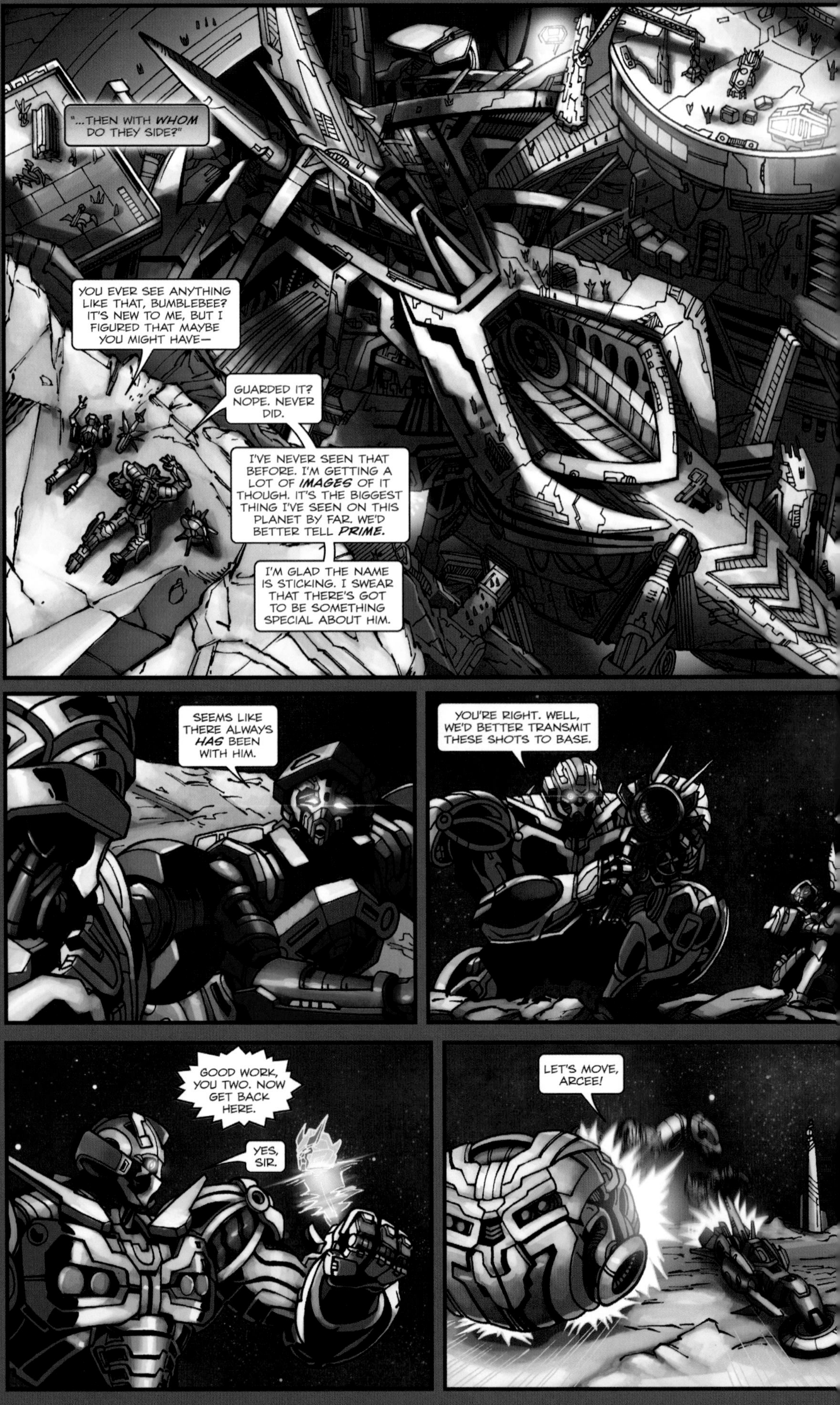
"...THEN WITH *WHOM* DO THEY SIDE?"
YOU EVER SEE ANYTHING LIKE THAT, BUMBLEBEE? IT'S NEW TO ME, BUT I FIGURED THAT MAYBE YOU MIGHT HAVE—
GUARDED IT? NOPE. NEVER DID.
I'VE NEVER SEEN THAT BEFORE. I'M GETTING A LOT OF *IMAGES* OF IT THOUGH. IT'S THE BIGGEST THING I'VE SEEN ON THIS PLANET BY FAR. WE'D BETTER TELL *PRIME.*
I'M GLAD THE NAME IS STICKING. I SWEAR THAT THERE'S GOT TO BE SOMETHING SPECIAL ABOUT HIM.
SEEMS LIKE THERE ALWAYS *HAS* BEEN WITH HIM.
YOU'RE RIGHT. WELL, WE'D BETTER TRANSMIT THESE SHOTS TO BASE.
GOOD WORK, YOU TWO. NOW GET BACK HERE.
YES, SIR.
LET'S MOVE, ARCEE!

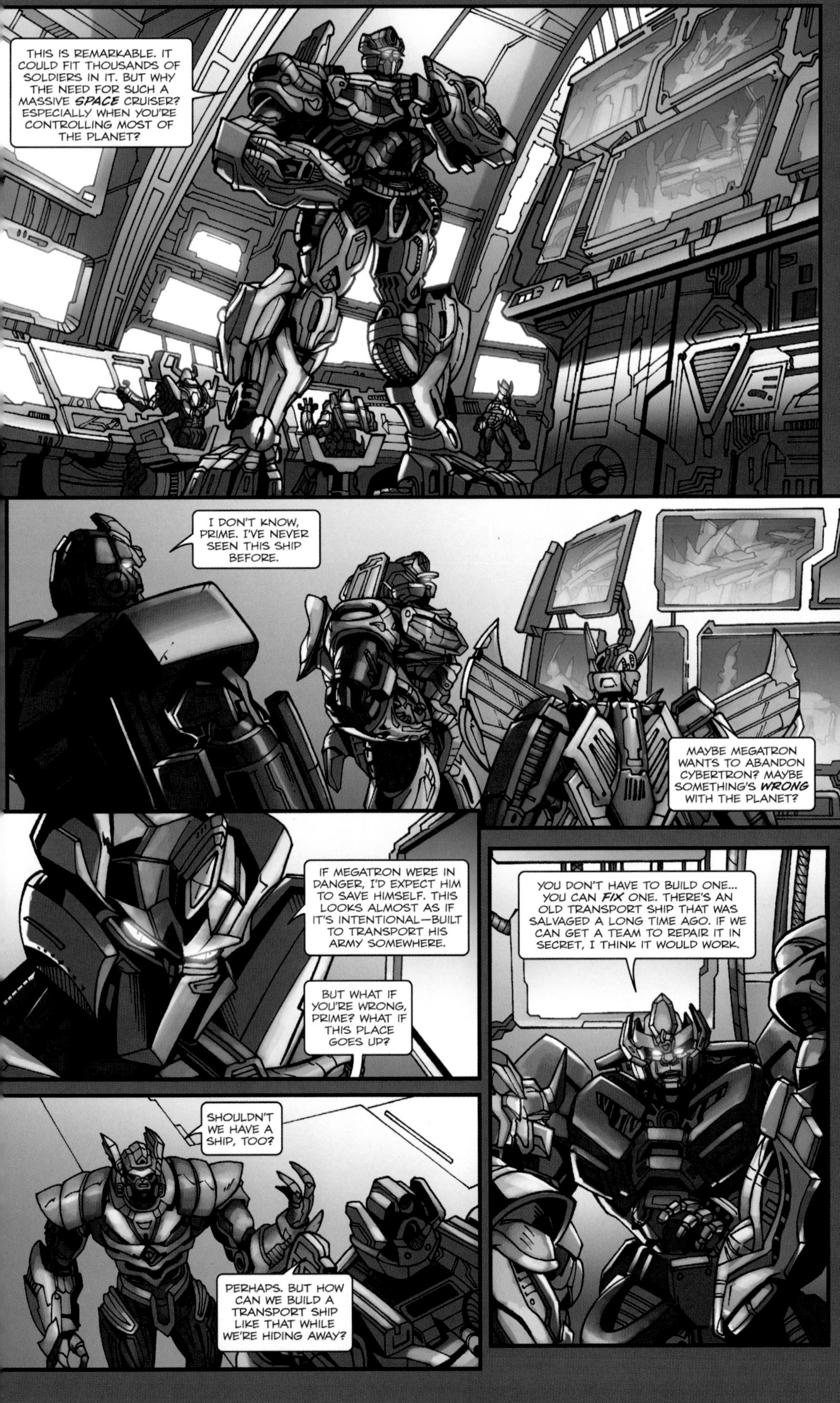
THIS IS REMARKABLE. IT COULD FIT THOUSANDS OF SOLDIERS IN IT. BUT WHY THE NEED FOR SUCH A MASSIVE SPACE CRUISER? ESPECIALLY WHEN YOU'RE CONTROLLING MOST OF THE PLANET?
I DON'T KNOW, PRIME. I'VE NEVER SEEN THIS SHIP BEFORE.
MAYBE MEGATRON WANTS TO ABANDON CYBERTRON? MAYBE SOMETHING'S WRONG WITH THE PLANET?
IF MEGATRON WERE IN DANGER, I'D EXPECT HIM TO SAVE HIMSELF. THIS LOOKS ALMOST AS IF IT'S INTENTIONAL—BUILT TO TRANSPORT HIS ARMY SOMEWHERE.
BUT WHAT IF YOU'RE WRONG, PRIME? WHAT IF THIS PLACE GOES UP?
SHOULDN'T WE HAVE A SHIP, TOO?
PERHAPS. BUT HOW CAN WE BUILD A TRANSPORT SHIP LIKE THAT WHILE WE'RE HIDING AWAY?
YOU DON'T HAVE TO BUILD ONE... YOU CAN FIX ONE. THERE'S AN OLD TRANSPORT SHIP THAT WAS SALVAGED A LONG TIME AGO. IF WE CAN GET A TEAM TO REPAIR IT IN SECRET, I THINK IT WOULD WORK.

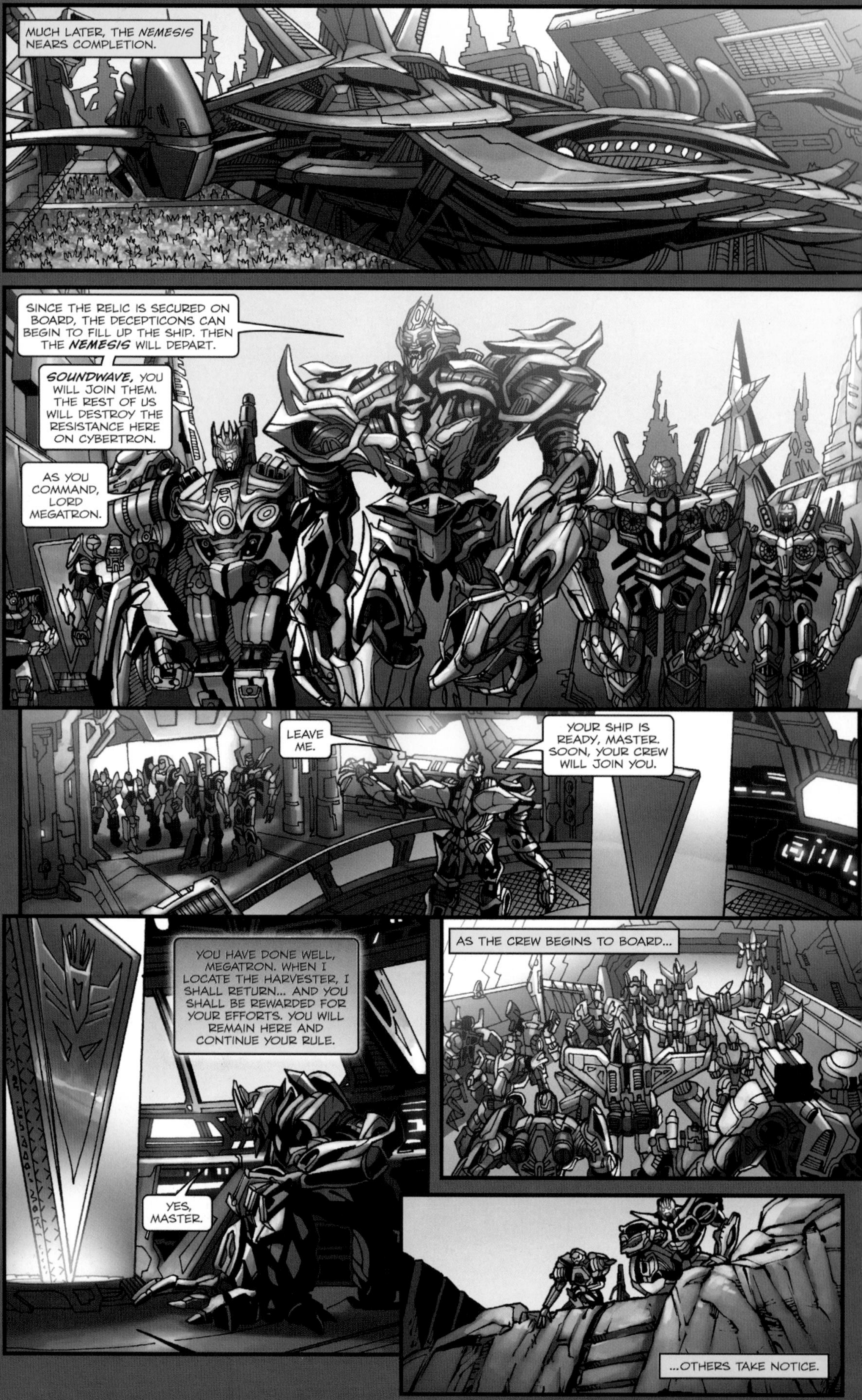
MUCH LATER, THE NEMESIS NEARS COMPLETION.
SINCE THE RELIC IS SECURED ON BOARD, THE DECEPTICONS CAN BEGIN TO FILL UP THE SHIP. THEN THE NEMESIS WILL DEPART.
SOUNDWAVE, YOU WILL JOIN THEM. THE REST OF US WILL DESTROY THE RESISTANCE HERE ON CYBERTRON.
AS YOU COMMAND, LORD MEGATRON.
LEAVE ME.
YOUR SHIP IS READY, MASTER. SOON, YOUR CREW WILL JOIN YOU.
YOU HAVE DONE WELL, MEGATRON. WHEN I LOCATE THE HARVESTER, I SHALL RETURN... AND YOU SHALL BE REWARDED FOR YOUR EFFORTS. YOU WILL REMAIN HERE AND CONTINUE YOUR RULE.
YES, MASTER.
AS THE CREW BEGINS TO BOARD...
...OTHERS TAKE NOTICE.

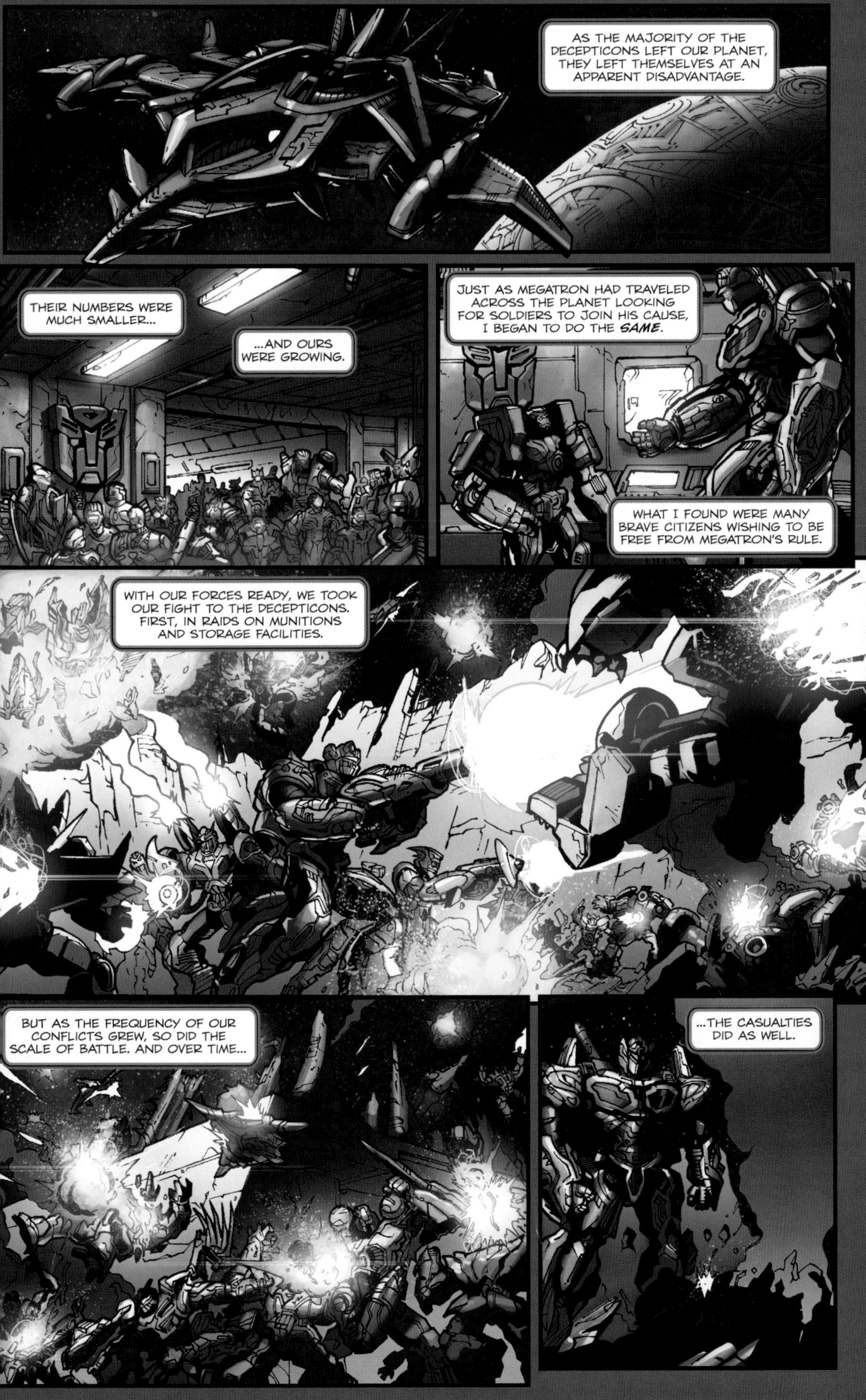
AS THE MAJORITY OF THE DECEPTICONS LEFT OUR PLANET, THEY LEFT THEMSELVES AT AN APPARENT DISADVANTAGE.
THEIR NUMBERS WERE MUCH SMALLER...
...AND OURS WERE GROWING.
JUST AS MEGATRON HAD TRAVELED ACROSS THE PLANET LOOKING FOR SOLDIERS TO JOIN HIS CAUSE, I BEGAN TO DO THE *SAME*.
WHAT I FOUND WERE MANY BRAVE CITIZENS WISHING TO BE FREE FROM MEGATRON'S RULE.
WITH OUR FORCES READY, WE TOOK OUR FIGHT TO THE DECEPTICONS. FIRST, IN RAIDS ON MUNITIONS AND STORAGE FACILITIES.
BUT AS THE FREQUENCY OF OUR CONFLICTS GREW, SO DID THE SCALE OF BATTLE. AND OVER TIME...
...THE CASUALTIES DID AS WELL.

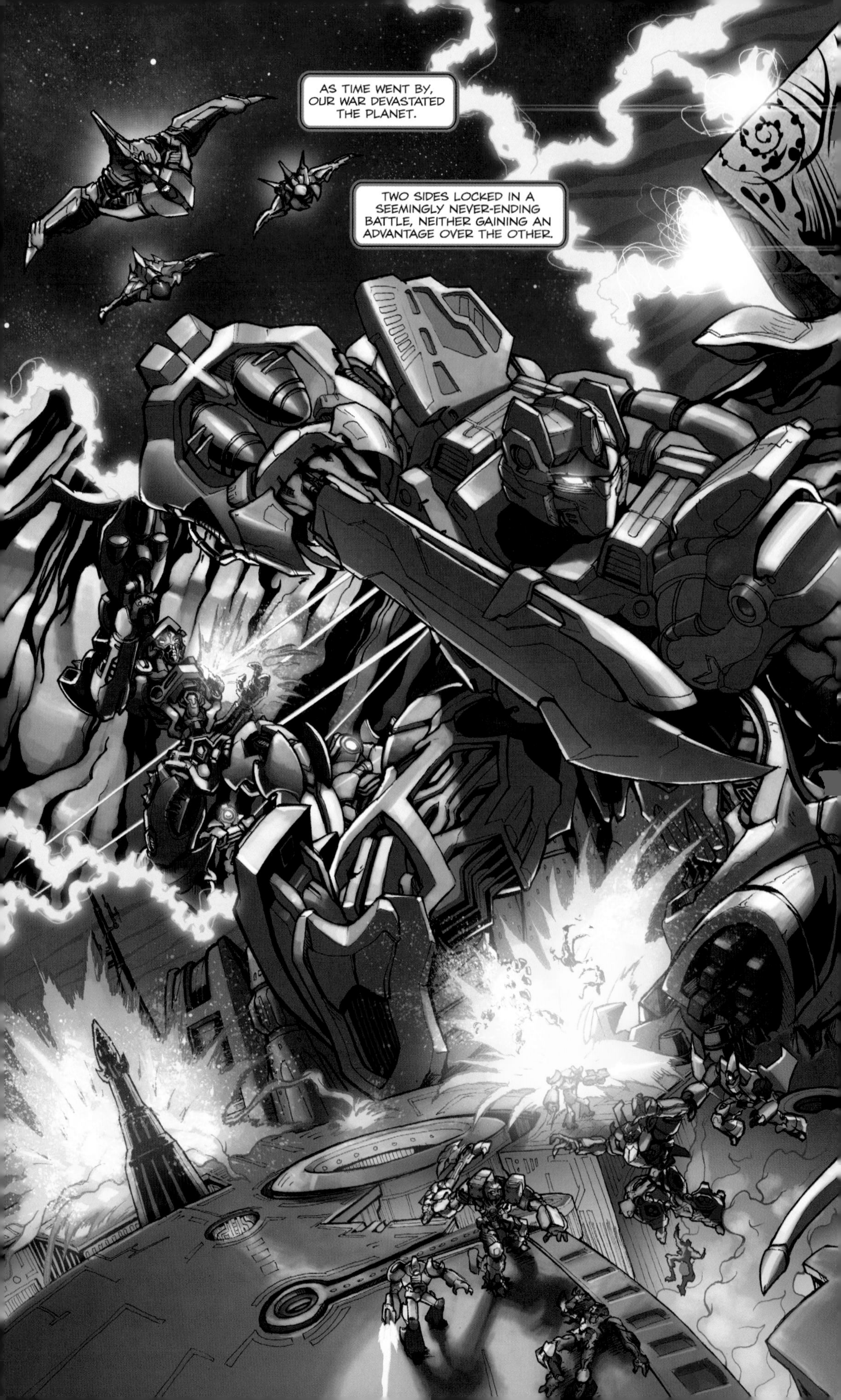
AS TIME WENT BY, OUR WAR DEVASTATED THE PLANET.
TWO SIDES LOCKED IN A SEEMINGLY NEVER-ENDING BATTLE, NEITHER GAINING AN ADVANTAGE OVER THE OTHER.

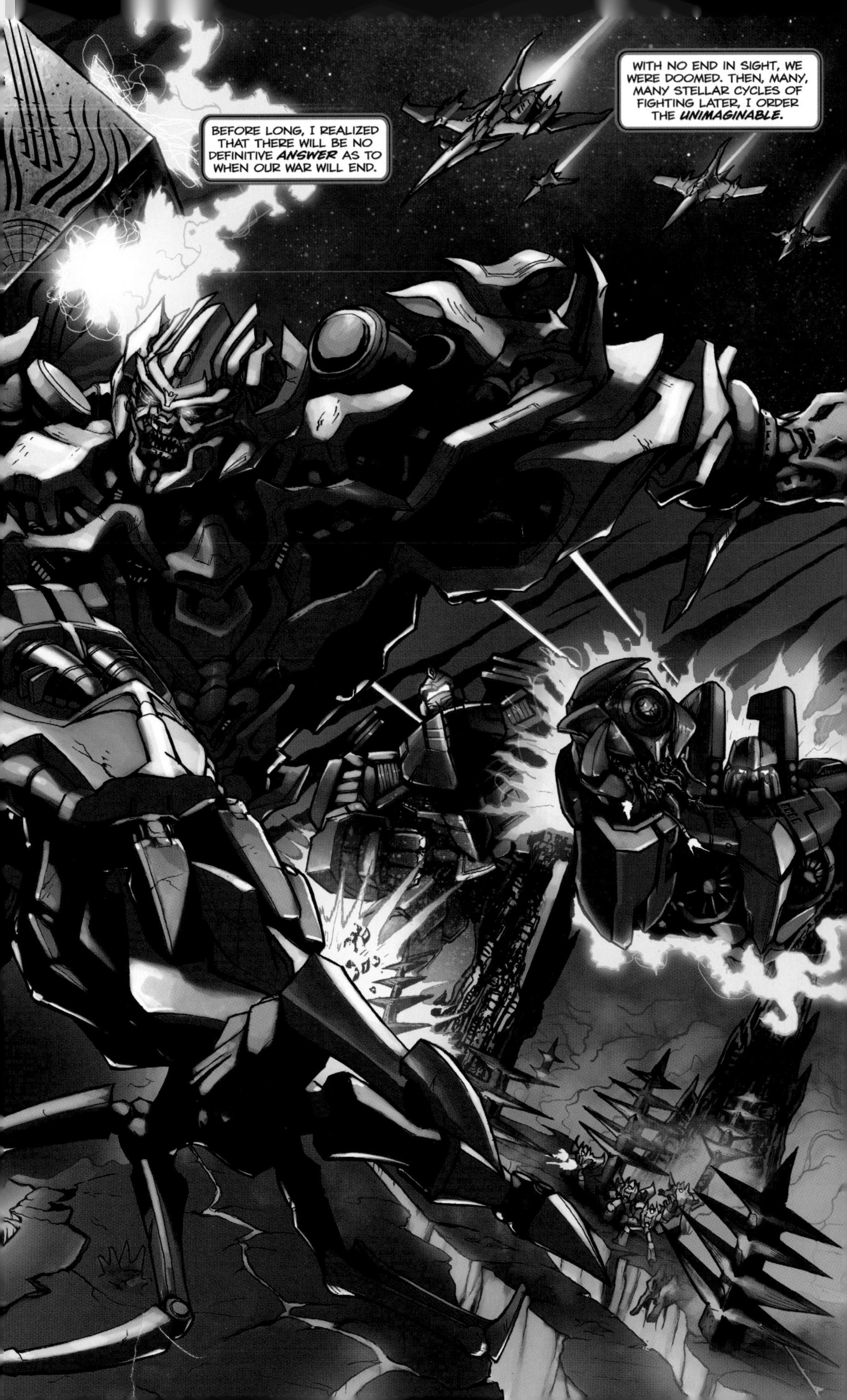
BEFORE LONG, I REALIZED THAT THERE WILL BE NO DEFINITIVE ANSWER AS TO WHEN OUR WAR WILL END.
WITH NO END IN SIGHT, WE WERE DOOMED. THEN, MANY, MANY STELLAR CYCLES OF FIGHTING LATER, I ORDER THE UNIMAGINABLE.

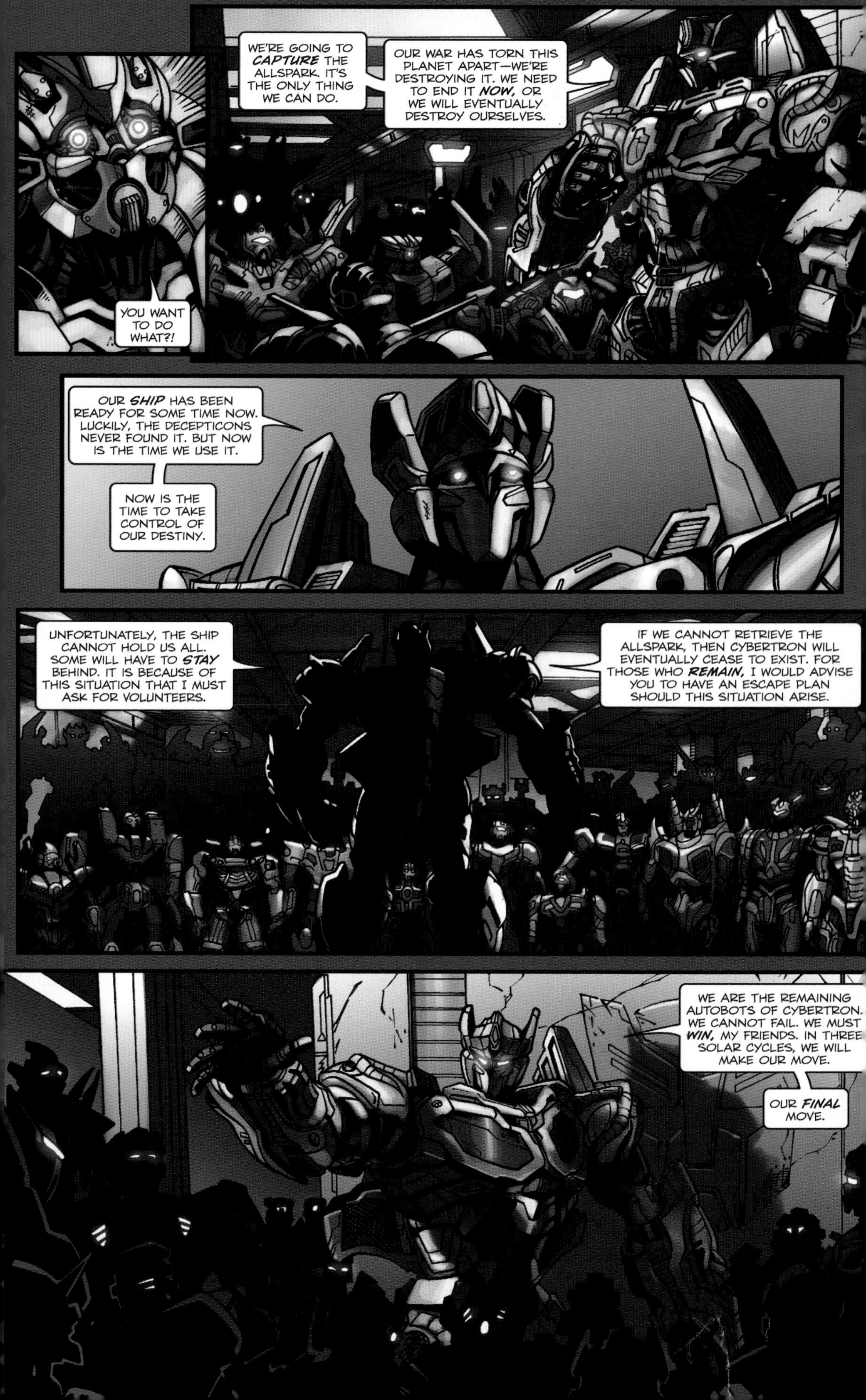

WE'RE GOING TO CAPTURE THE ALLSPARK. IT'S THE ONLY THING WE CAN DO.
OUR WAR HAS TORN THIS PLANET APART—WE'RE DESTROYING IT. WE NEED TO END IT NOW, OR WE WILL EVENTUALLY DESTROY OURSELVES.
YOU WANT TO DO WHAT?!
OUR SHIP HAS BEEN READY FOR SOME TIME NOW. LUCKILY, THE DECEPTICONS NEVER FOUND IT. BUT NOW IS THE TIME WE USE IT.
NOW IS THE TIME TO TAKE CONTROL OF OUR DESTINY.
UNFORTUNATELY, THE SHIP CANNOT HOLD US ALL. SOME WILL HAVE TO STAY BEHIND. IT IS BECAUSE OF THIS SITUATION THAT I MUST ASK FOR VOLUNTEERS.
IF WE CANNOT RETRIEVE THE ALLSPARK, THEN CYBERTRON WILL EVENTUALLY CEASE TO EXIST. FOR THOSE WHO REMAIN, I WOULD ADVISE YOU TO HAVE AN ESCAPE PLAN SHOULD THIS SITUATION ARISE.
WE ARE THE REMAINING AUTOBOTS OF CYBERTRON. WE CANNOT FAIL. WE MUST WIN, MY FRIENDS. IN THREE SOLAR CYCLES, WE WILL MAKE OUR MOVE.
OUR FINAL MOVE.

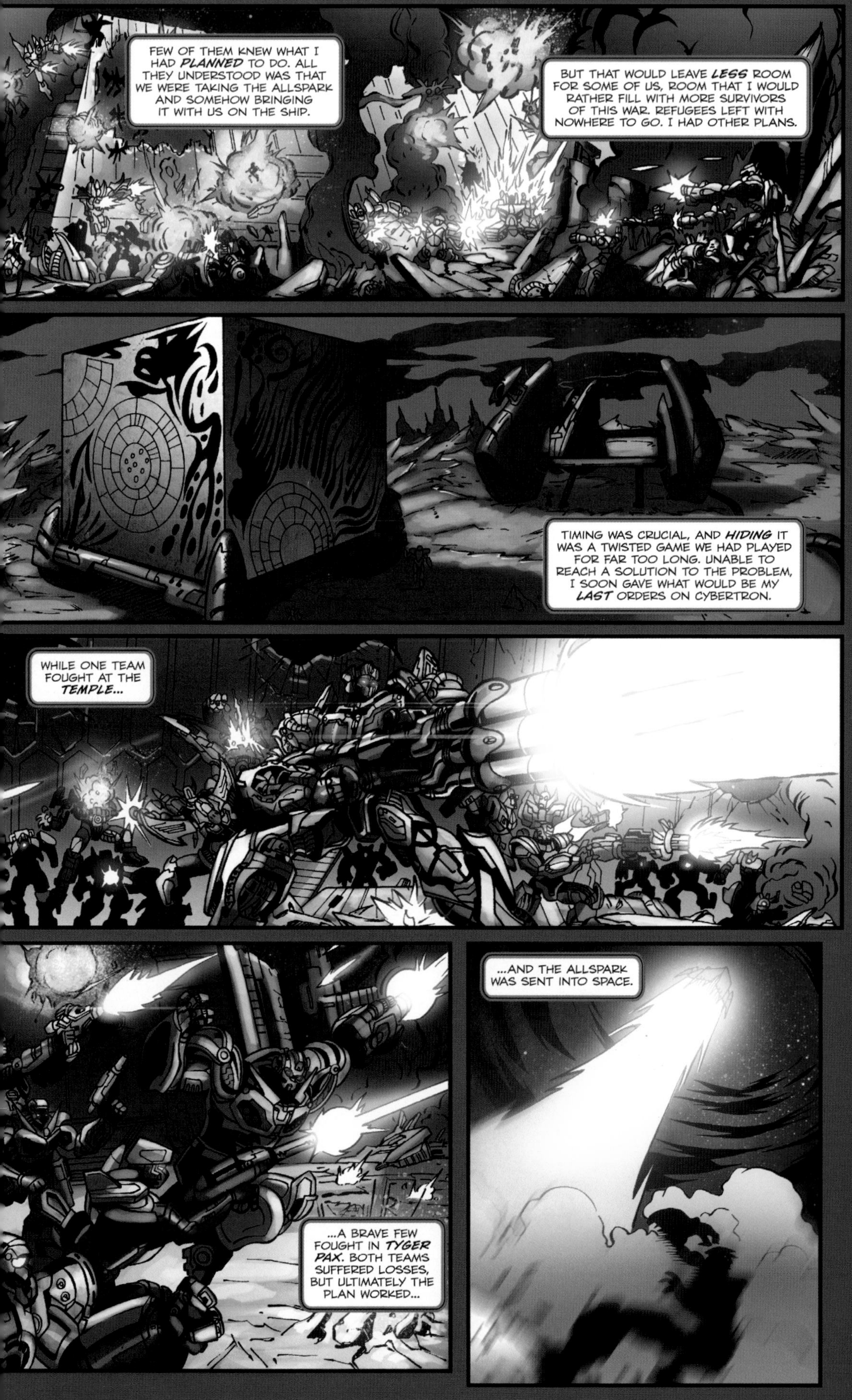

FEW OF THEM KNEW WHAT I HAD PLANNED TO DO. ALL THEY UNDERSTOOD WAS THAT WE WERE TAKING THE ALLSPARK AND SOMEHOW BRINGING IT WITH US ON THE SHIP.
BUT THAT WOULD LEAVE LESS ROOM FOR SOME OF US, ROOM THAT I WOULD RATHER FILL WITH MORE SURVIVORS OF THIS WAR. REFUGEES LEFT WITH NOWHERE TO GO. I HAD OTHER PLANS.
TIMING WAS CRUCIAL, AND HIDING IT WAS A TWISTED GAME WE HAD PLAYED FOR FAR TOO LONG. UNABLE TO REACH A SOLUTION TO THE PROBLEM, I SOON GAVE WHAT WOULD BE MY LAST ORDERS ON CYBERTRON.
WHILE ONE TEAM FOUGHT AT THE TEMPLE...
...A BRAVE FEW FOUGHT IN TYGER PAX. BOTH TEAMS SUFFERED LOSSES, BUT ULTIMATELY THE PLAN WORKED...
...AND THE ALLSPARK WAS SENT INTO SPACE.

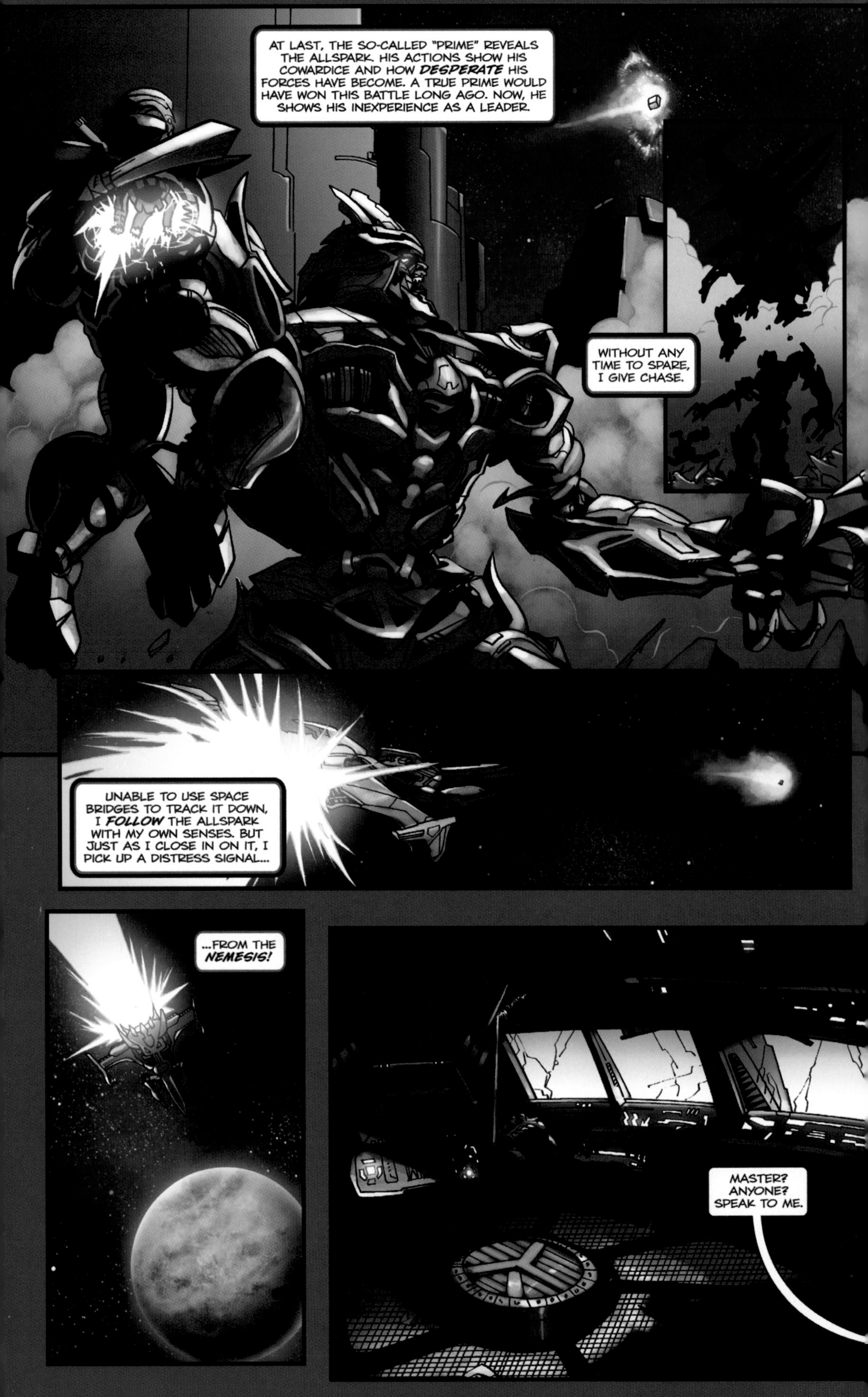
AT LAST, THE SO-CALLED "PRIME" REVEALS THE ALLSPARK. HIS ACTIONS SHOW HIS COWARDICE AND HOW DESPERATE HIS FORCES HAVE BECOME. A TRUE PRIME WOULD HAVE WON THIS BATTLE LONG AGO. NOW, HE SHOWS HIS INEXPERIENCE AS A LEADER.
WITHOUT ANY TIME TO SPARE, I GIVE CHASE.
UNABLE TO USE SPACE BRIDGES TO TRACK IT DOWN, I FOLLOW THE ALLSPARK WITH MY OWN SENSES. BUT JUST AS I CLOSE IN ON IT, I PICK UP A DISTRESS SIGNAL...
...FROM THE NEMESIS!
MASTER? ANYONE? SPEAK TO ME.

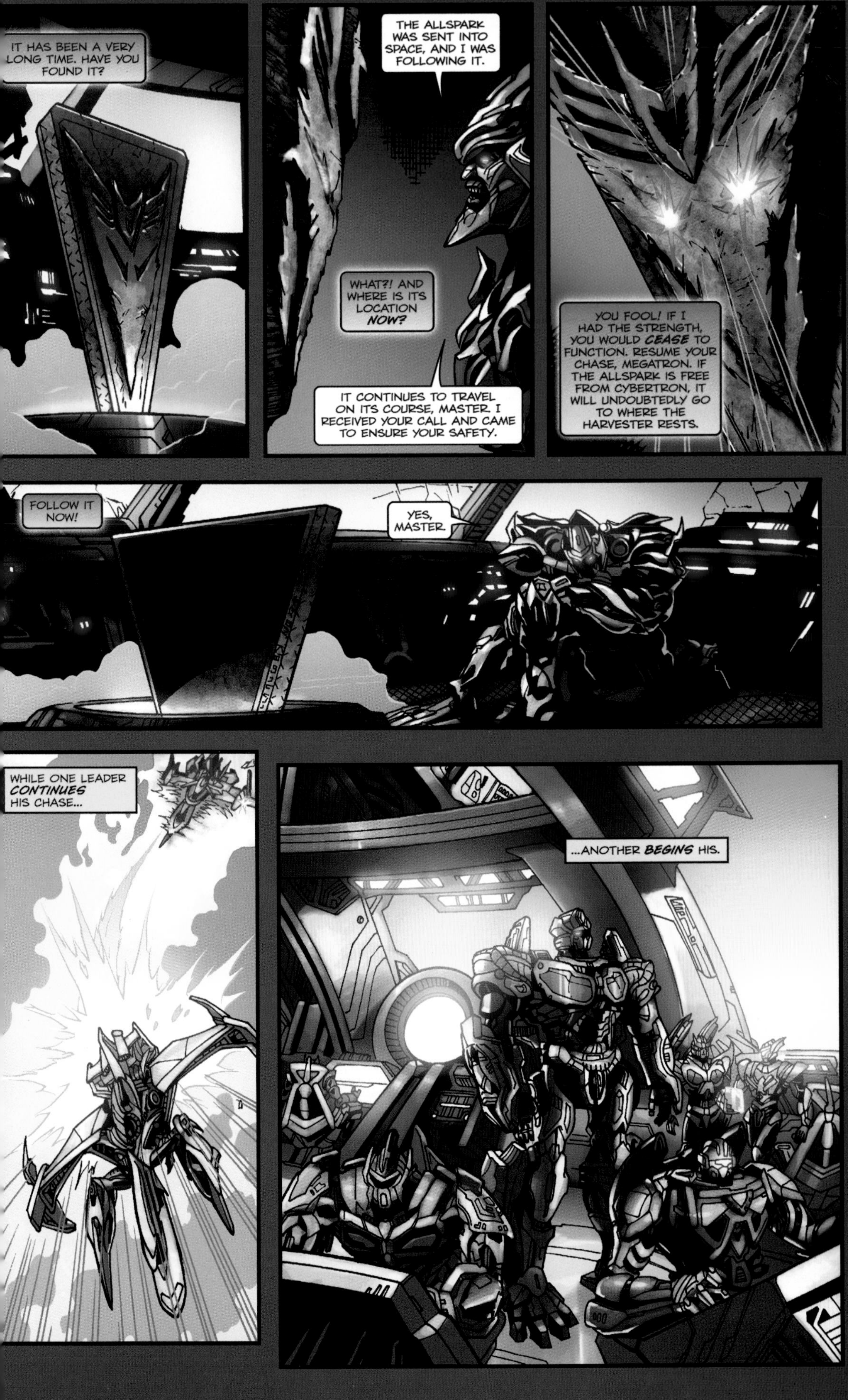
IT HAS BEEN A VERY LONG TIME. HAVE YOU FOUND IT?
THE ALLSPARK WAS SENT INTO SPACE, AND I WAS FOLLOWING IT.
WHAT?! AND WHERE IS ITS LOCATION NOW?
IT CONTINUES TO TRAVEL ON ITS COURSE, MASTER. I RECEIVED YOUR CALL AND CAME TO ENSURE YOUR SAFETY.
YOU FOOL! IF I HAD THE STRENGTH, YOU WOULD CEASE TO FUNCTION. RESUME YOUR CHASE, MEGATRON. IF THE ALLSPARK IS FREE FROM CYBERTRON, IT WILL UNDOUBTEDLY GO TO WHERE THE HARVESTER RESTS.
FOLLOW IT NOW!
YES, MASTER.
WHILE ONE LEADER CONTINUES HIS CHASE...
...ANOTHER BEGINS HIS.

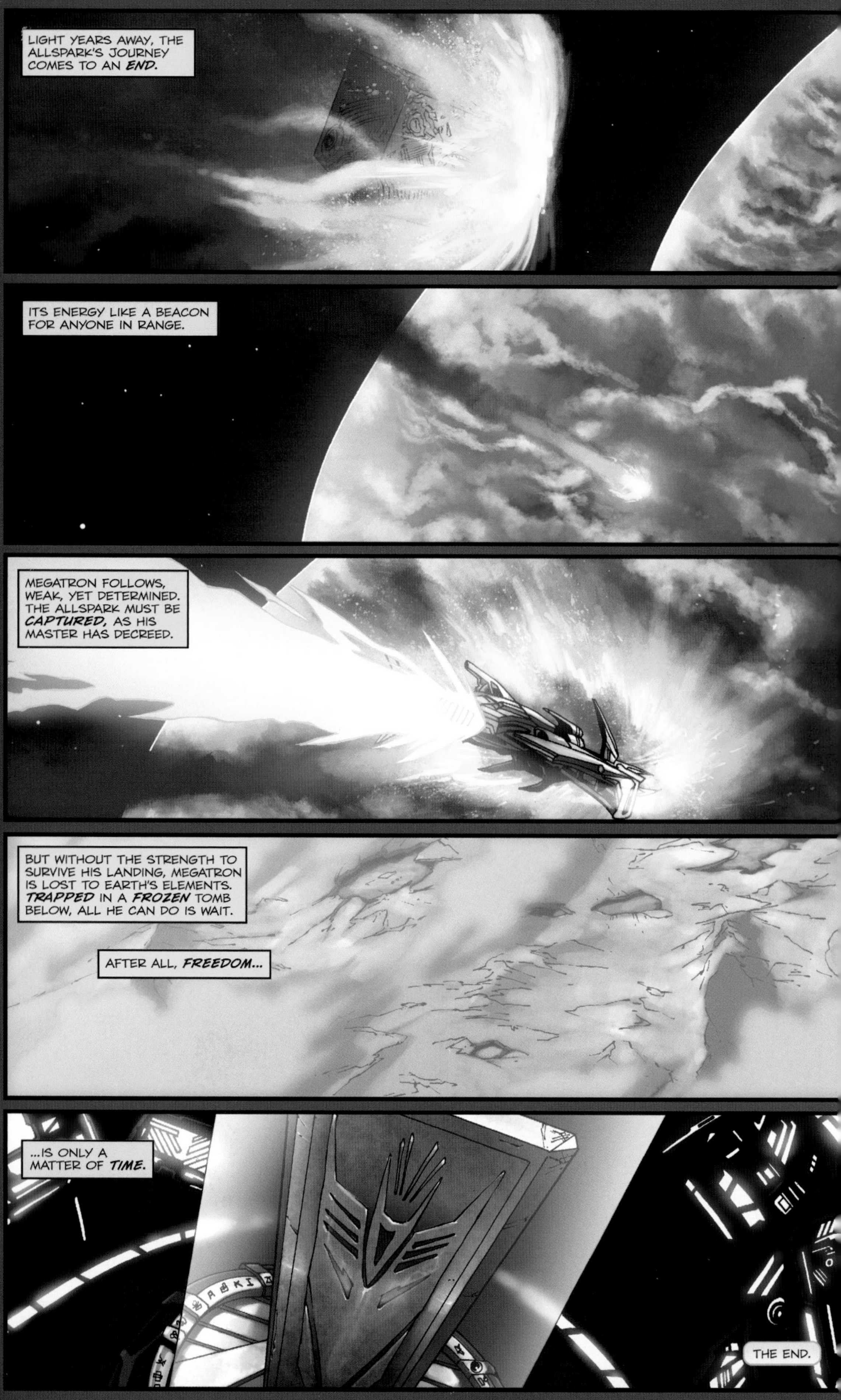
LIGHT YEARS AWAY, THE ALLSPARK'S JOURNEY COMES TO AN *END*.
ITS ENERGY LIKE A BEACON FOR ANYONE IN RANGE.
MEGATRON FOLLOWS, WEAK, YET DETERMINED. THE ALLSPARK MUST BE *CAPTURED,* AS HIS MASTER HAS DECREED.
BUT WITHOUT THE STRENGTH TO SURVIVE HIS LANDING, MEGATRON IS LOST TO EARTH'S ELEMENTS. *TRAPPED* IN A *FROZEN* TOMB BELOW, ALL HE CAN DO IS WAIT.
AFTER ALL, *FREEDOM*...
...IS ONLY A MATTER OF *TIME*.
THE END.